To _____,

THE POWER IS IN YOU
THERE'S NOTHING YOU CAN'T DO
AS LONG AS YOU STAY TRUE
TO THE POWER THAT'S IN YOU

Love,
Alexander, Jonah,
Elise, & Eagan.

We are committed to giving back. By supporting Trustfall Collaborations, you are supporting many causes we believe in. Join us today, and let's be the change we hope to see in the world— together! We pledge to donate 10% of proceeds to the following worthy causes, uniquely chosen for this project.
Action Against Hunger; Big Brothers Big Sisters of America; Creative Action; El Patojismo; Feeding America; Hip 2B Square; Just Keep Livin Foundation; Malachi Destiny & Purpose; NEDA; Starship Foundation.
Please visit www.trustfallcollaborations.com/tcgives to find out more & give today!

Library of Congress Cataloging in Publication Data
Names: Alexander Hiers & Jonah Fujikawa, Trustfall Collaborations
Title: Elf E. Ramone

Summary: A new story in the folklore of the holiday season.
The tale of the elf who started the tradition of leaving cookies and milk for Santa Claus.

Special thanks: Damion & the Square family, Conleigh Jackson & the Punkin' family, my loving Hiers kin, the Fujikawa fam, the VCS 8, Allison Price, Joe Carter, the Whitson & Anderson/Campbell clans, Kankana Basu, the Overstreet family, Dave & the amazing Rambler team.

TRUSTFALL
COLLABORATIONS

www.trustfallcollaborations.com
ISBN 978-1-66781-131-4

Subjects: Stories in rhyme; Holidays- fiction; Imagination- fiction; Holiday folklore- fiction; Christmas- fiction; Self- acceptance - fiction; Diversity -fiction; Children's literature -fiction; Children's Multiculturalism- fiction; Summer- fiction; Winter- fiction; Summer Solstice - fiction; Community- fiction; Baking; Baking with Kids; Recipe book; Hardcover- fiction; Holidays and Celebrations- fiction.

ELF E. RAMONE

Written by: Alexander Hiers,
Jonah Fujikawa, Elise Isabella

Illustrated by: Eagan Tilghman

Story by: Alexander Hiers
Director of Photography: Joey Bazan

IN COLLABORATION WITH DAMION SQUARE

'Twas the day before the summer solstice
when all round Christmas Isle,
every creature was moving, working, stirring,
going the extra mile.

All elves, humans, animals, and birds
were planning Santa's stay.
For every year he'd vacation there,
to rest and catch sunrays.

Santa loved his summer holiday,
chilling in the Christmas Isle way.
This special place, with such magical cheer,
brought some of his favorite days of the year.

On the peninsula of Christmas Isle,
with binoculars you could see
(it wasn't too near, but wasn't too far)
a small cabin with a chimney . . .

There, the youngest of the Ramone family,
Eugenio Ramone (folks called him Elf E.)
was playing pretend, alone—
sitting high up on his throne.

The older Ramones planned their most
famous, divine, delicious feast,
to fill St. Nick up from head to toe—
stuffed within his red wool fleece.

Outside, Elf E.'s siblings dug a sandpit
for cooking their feast on the beach,
looking forward to Santa's grand arrival,
and his jolly, joyous speech.

"I'm the pitmaster!" his papa roared loud,
sounding like an alarm.
When he saw Elf E. just sitting around,
he dragged him out by the arm.

Dipping and dodging past pots and pans,
and all the family,
his mom swung her limbs, directing them,
as they worked skillfully.

Hopeful, Elf E. bravely asked his papa,
"May I join the festivities today?"
Papa Rafa Ramone quickly said,
"No. Santa is coming. We work. No play."

On the sand dunes beyond his siblings,
back down along the shore,
Elf E. saw the other kids playing
games he'd been longing for.

Elf E. questioned aloud,
"Please! Can't you make an exception, just one?!"
Papa Rafa growled,
"You can go when the work is good and done."

Across the shoreline of the beach,
kiddos stretched their arms—reach, reach, reach!
Elves were laid flat out on their backs,
flapping their arms and legs like bats.

"Look, look, look, we made sand angels!" they giggled.
Then they drew a crown on the one in the middle.
Some, building sandcastles, shaped and fiddled.
Some sat down with books of rhymes and riddles.

A sandman rode by on top of a cooler,
wearing sunglasses and looking peculiar.
He had buttons fashioned from seashells,
and a coat with dripping gold lapels.

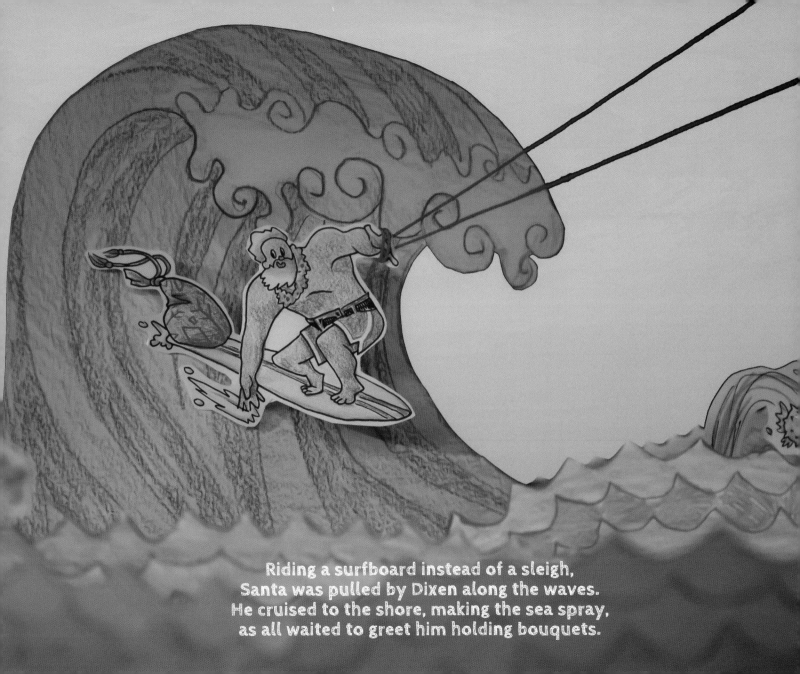

Riding a surfboard instead of a sleigh,
Santa was pulled by Dixen along the waves.
He cruised to the shore, making the sea spray,
as all waited to greet him holding bouquets.

Echoing over the waves and through the hills,
Santa's song began, giving everyone chills.
Santa Claus sang, "HO-HO-HO-liday time!"
"Here comes Santa Claus," the elves sang in reply.

Santa jumped off his surfboard.
He tumbled and somersaulted into the grand horde.
JINGLE, WHOOSH, DING, RING, and SPLASH!
They ran so fast toward him, they almost got whiplash.

He showered them all with candy snowflakes—
the Christmas treats everyone loves and craves.
Santa laughed with new and old friends, getting winded,
but making time for all, until the line ended.

Miles away and craning to snoop,
Elf E., from the peninsula, tried to see.
But Santa was hidden by the group,
drowning in the warmth of a crowded sea.

Santa stood tall and, clearing his throat,
declared, "Attention, Christmas Isle folks!
Time to sign up for the yearly competition,
where you get to show me your best invention."

"About the winner's gift, the whole world will be told,
and the winner gets a ticket to the North Pole!"
Santa hung a list for all to sign up,
and hoped for a large turn up.

So creatures lined up, stretched to the isle's end,
chattering about what it takes to win.
Word spread near, then far throughout the island—
whispers traveled towards Elf E. on the wind . . .

Elf E. heard, and did a little dance.
"This is my moment, my big chance."
He was filled with glee immediately.
"An inventor is what I want to be!"

Elf E. tried just once more to ask,
"May I take part in the competition?"
Papa Rafa thought of the task . . .
"Maybe. First, complete the family mission!"

Elf E. knew that he should wait.
His papa's rules he shouldn't disobey.
But this chance couldn't be missed,
so he snuck out and signed up on the list!

"Elf Eugenio Ramone,"
he wrote proudly and with hope.
"My chance to create and play . . .
Today is the greatest day!"

Elf E. snuck back to his home,
and worked like he was never even gone.
For to be a true Ramone,
you must never quit till the job is done.

As the Ramones finished up their work,
Elf E. helped them clean.
He thought to save the extra spices,
all while he daydreamed . . .

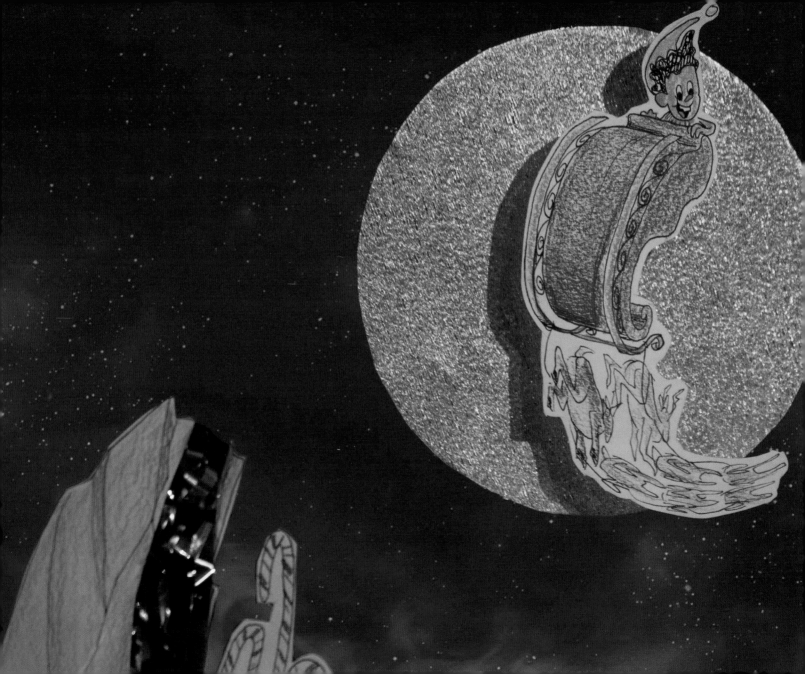

A winter wonderland!
The Tinsel Falls at Jack Frost Lagoon!
The elves' workshop!
Riding in Santa's sleigh, traveling past the moon!

Thoughts floated in his mind like
snowflakes at the North Pole.
What perfect idea would help
Elf E. reach his big goal?

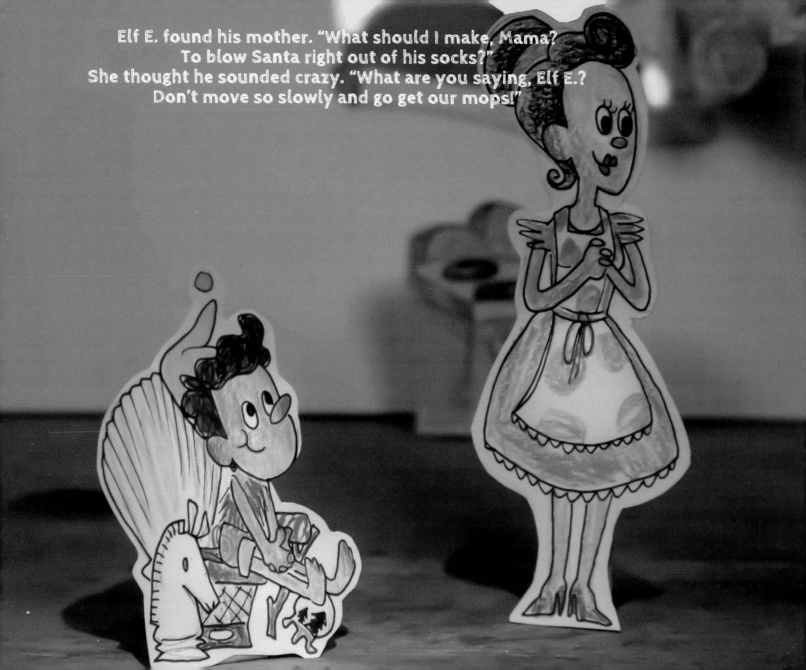

Elf E. found his mother. "What should I make, Mama?
To blow Santa right out of his socks?"
She thought he sounded crazy. "What are you saying, Elf E.?
Don't move so slowly and go get our mops!"

Then in the afternoon, instead of taking his siesta,
Elf E. went to his hideout to prepare for the fiesta.
Tucked away was his thinking spot,
where grand ideas were born and caught . . .

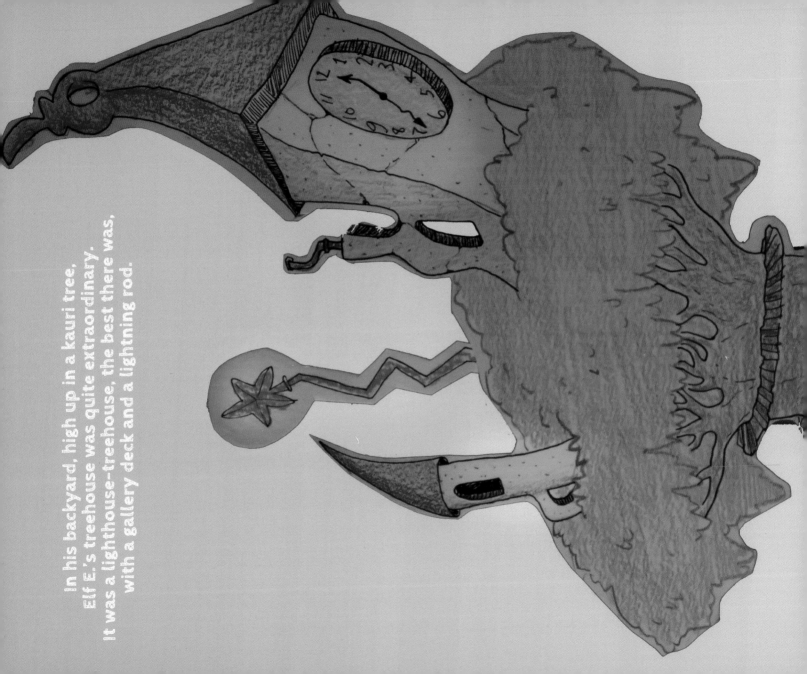

In his backyard, high up in a kauri tree,
Elf E.'s treehouse was quite extraordinary.
It was a lighthouse-treehouse, the best there was,
with a gallery deck and a lightning rod.

Elf E. imagined, invented, created,
seeking an idea, perfect and clear.
He scribbled his thoughts, then crumpled them up—
such an idea just wouldn't appear!

Oh! He was nearly in tears.
Then, with patience and all ears,
his abuelita popped in with spiced chai.
She'd brought Elf E. a drink, to be kind.

Abuelita stayed a short while for a chat.
But when Elf E. put some spices in a hat,
and stirred them around with a baseball bat,
Abuelita gasped!

Eyes wide with wonder,
she stooped in and asked,
"What are you doing, my silly boy?
Those are not for work, they're just toys!"

But Elf E. twirled about without a single care,
as cinnamon and nutmeg smells filled the air.
He added some milk, sugar, eggs, and some clove,
and a dash of the secret ingredient—

Elf E. baked a whole flan in the blink of an eye!
And, in just one bite, they knew they couldn't deny . . .
"Wow!" Abuelita gushed, "This is delicious!
A chef this good shouldn't have to do dishes."

Elf E. laughed, then blurted out,
"Oh! Abuelita, that's it!
Our family recipes,
they're famous—always a hit!"

So Elf E. mixed and whipped,
then he scraped and he baked.
There was no time to lean,
it was time to be seen!

Elf E. worked hard, very late through the night,
till he fell asleep under his lamplight.
Up high in his lighthouse-treehouse,
Elf E. slept, quiet as a mouse.

Ding ding! The bells began ringing,
and the solstice birds were singing.
Elf E. yawned wide, and slowly awoke
to see his mess of baking and notes.

And then he saw a present next to him.
"To: A great chef. From: All your loving kin!
We're so very proud of you, Son. We know what you have done.
We'll be there for you. When it's time, we know just what to do."

Such magic on this magnificent day!
Thankful, he unwrapped it without delay.
He saw it was all he'd ever wanted—
a chef's hat! Custom. Unique. Unwonted.

Ding ding! The Christmas Isle clock continued to chime out . . .
which meant it was time to compete. Elf E. had no doubts!
So he tied a bow around Santa's gift,
put on his chef's hat, and called for a lift.

Elf E. entered the competition hall feeling nervous.
Courage came knowing he was there to show them his purpose.
Sweaty palms, trembling, and a racing heart
meant he really wanted to wow with his art.

The competition kicked off—such great creations!
Each presentation raised Santa's expectations.
A doll that could do somersaults, a dress made out of nuts and bolts,
a device to fatten your smile, a toy car faster than a child.

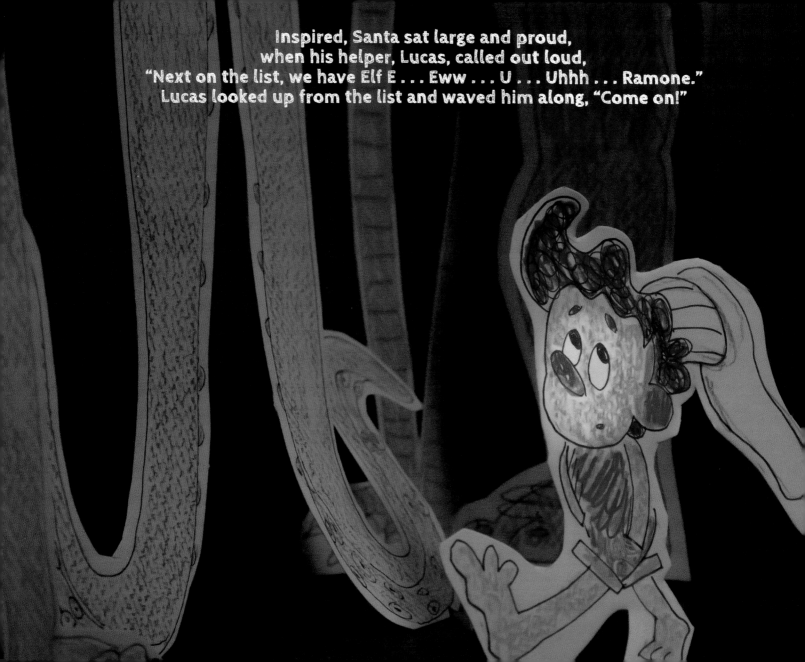

Inspired, Santa sat large and proud,
when his helper, Lucas, called out loud,
"Next on the list, we have Elf E . . . Eww . . . U . . . Uhhh . . . Ramone."
Lucas looked up from the list and waved him along, "Come on!"

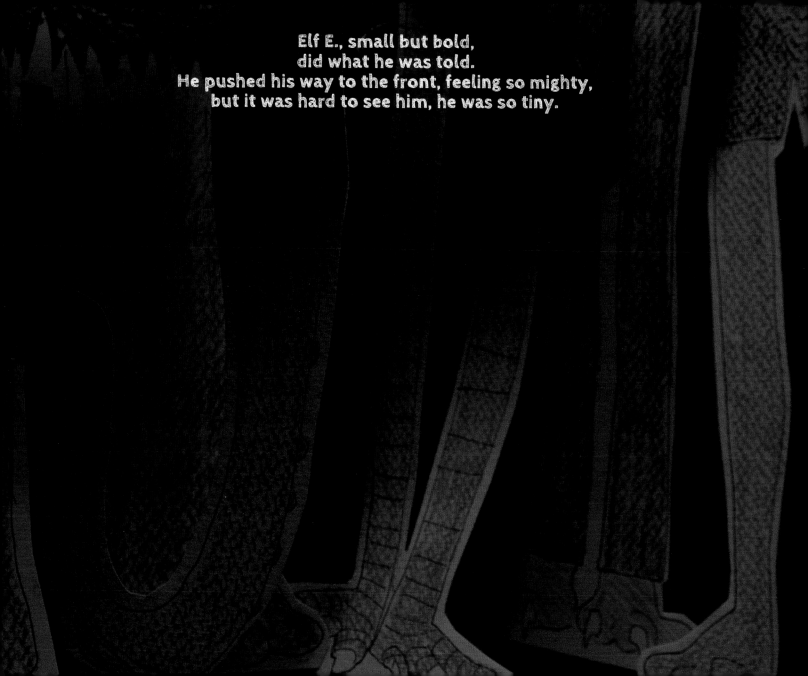

Elf E., small but bold,
did what he was told.
He pushed his way to the front, feeling so mighty,
but it was hard to see him, he was so tiny.

Hello, Mister Santa Claus. My name is Eugenio . . . call me Lil' E.
Umm . . . and my papa always taught me,
'It's better to give than to receive'.
Mama makes a list of what she's thankful for on every holiday's eve."

"For me, they are the reason.
My family makes the holidays a magical season.
We work hard, but we laugh as we cook. It gives me a warm, happy feeling.
Our home is endlessly filled with love, right from the floor up to the ceiling."

Right then, Papa walked in with a hot
Horchata Cocoa Latte Dream.
It had gold and cinnamon sprinkled
on a giant mountain of whipped cream.

Abuelita brought her very special flan on a plate,
and sang so the magic of the moment would resonate.
Mama brought in handmade napkins of fine mulberry silk.
And finally, Elf E. revealed his gift to Santa—

cookies

and

milk.

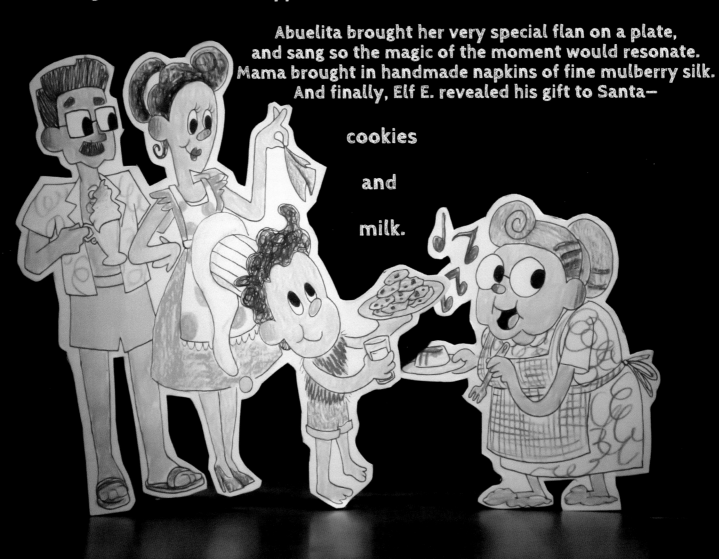

You bring us all presents," Elf E. said, "but there's none for you,
so I thought of something simple that all families can do.
They can make or bake their favorite treat,
and leave something special for you to eat."

Santa took a giant gulp and bite.
His eyes lit up in utter delight.
And through his now-milky moustache (which made him laugh),
Santa cheered, "Two, four, six, eight, dig in, don't wait!"

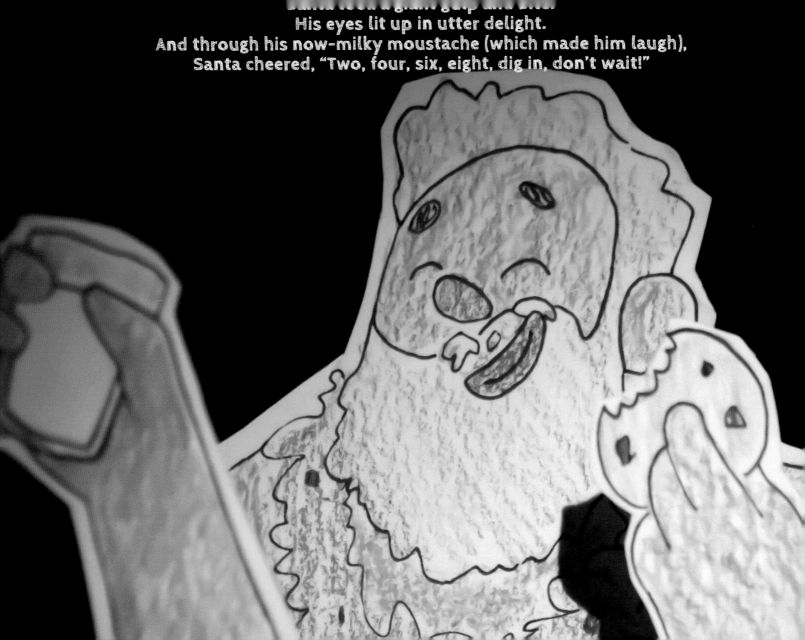

Not a single drop or crumb remained,
they all had their fill.
"And now, the winner," Santa proclaimed.
The big reveal . . .

Lucas handed Santa the results,
making everyone nervous (even the adults).
Santa dramatically opened the envelope,
and read it with a kaleidoscope.

"You were all quite wonderful and should be extremely proud.
But in this competition only one winner's allowed.
Everyone created, and shared, such magical treasures,
but one of you created something well beyond measure."

"And for the grand prize . . .
the ultimate goal . . .
you get to come with
me to the North Pole . . . "

"Elf E. Ramone!"

The crowd erupted as the winner was named.
"Sweet summer sunshine!!! We won!" Elf E. exclaimed.

Friends and family,
together, celebrated.
Love, joy, and peace,
the Ramones had created.

The story of Elf E. Ramone traveled far and fast.
The whole world gathered their families to have a blast!

Antigua, Guatemala

Meridian, Mississippi

Kigali, Rwanda

Auckland, New Zealand

LOVE.

Los Angeles, California

Austin, Texas

Sapporo, Japan

Flint, Michigan

And so Santa found, from that day forward, all the nice kiddos made him a treat.
At each and every house, they left him a gift—their favorite dessert to eat.

HAPPY HOLIDAYS!

YOUR FAMILY PHOTO HERE

ELF E.'S COOKIES
THE RECIPE

Duration:

Prep. time: 15-20 minutes
Cool time: 20 minutes
Bake time: 13-15 minutes
Total time: 55 minutes
Servings: 12-16 delicious cookies

Tools needed:

Kitchen towel
Large bowl
Measuring cups
Whisk
Measuring spoons
Baking tray
Oven mitts
Spatula
Plate
Drinking glasses

*(If using butter)
  Small microwave safe bowl

Ingredients:

¼ cup brown sugar (packed)
½ cup white sugar
½ teaspoon baking soda
2 ¼ teaspoons ground cinnamon
¼ teaspoon ground nutmeg
¼ teaspoon ground cloves
¼ teaspoon allspice
1 ½ cups flour
Pinch of salt
½ cup semi-sweet chocolate chips
Confectioners' sugar
½ cup shortening
*(or 1 stick unsalted butter)
2 teaspoons vanilla extract
1 egg
Canola spray or butter (to grease)
Milk (to drink)

Secret Ingredient:

Lots and lots of love

ELF E.'S COOKIES: INSTRUCTIONS

MIX IT
- Wash your hands.
- Gather your tools and ingredients.
- Measure and pour brown sugar and white sugar into your large bowl.
- Cut up the shortening into small pieces, and add to the bowl.
*if using butter instead of shortening, melt in your small bowl in the microwave for 30-40 seconds before adding to the large bowl.
- Using your whisk, mix the ingredients until evenly mixed.

GET CRACKIN'
- Add vanilla extract to your large bowl of ingredients.
- Crack the egg into the mixture. Throw away (or compost!) the shell, then wash your hands.
- Using your whisk, mix the new ingredients in. You're doing great!

TWIRL ABOUT WITHOUT A SINGLE CARE
- In your large bowl, add baking soda, cinnamon, nutmeg, cloves, and allspice. Whisk till the spices are evenly spread throughout the mixture.
- Add a pinch of salt, then add flour slowly and mix as you go.
- Add chocolate chips and fold into the dough, until they are evenly spread throughout.

HEAT UP & COOL DOWN
- Preheat the oven to 350 degrees fahrenheit. Hot! Hot! Hot!
- Put your bowl of magical deliciousness in the fridge for 20 minutes.
- Put your drinking glasses in the freezer.

SCRAPE IT
- Take your bowl out of the fridge. Cold! Cold! Cold!
- Grease your baking tray with canola oil spray or butter.
- Time to get messy! Use your hands to roll the dough into 12-16 balls. Place your cookie balls on the tray, evenly spaced apart.
- Wash your hands.

KEEP GOING! . . .

ELF E.'S COOKIES! INSTRUCTIONS

BAKE IT
- Put your oven mitts on, and slide your tray of cookies into the oven.
- Bake for 13-15 minutes, until golden brown.
- Smell the amazing flavors!

THE SECRET INGREDIENT
- Tell a family member you love them and why you're thankful for them.
- Give the cookies a word of encouragement.
- No time to lean, it's time to make the kitchen nice and clean.

YOUR INVENTION
- Time to be seen! Using your oven mitts, pull the cookies out of the oven.
(Be careful—Hot! Hot! Hot!)
- Turn off the oven.

LET IT SNOW
- Let your cookies cool on the tray for a few minutes.
- Careful, the tray is still hot, hot, hot!
- Remove cookies from the tray with your spatula, and move them to your plate.
- Sprinkle confectioners' sugar over the cookies like snow.

CELEBRATE
- Take the drinking glasses out of the freezer. Fill with your favorite milk.
- Leave one drinking glass of milk, and some cookies, for Santa Claus.

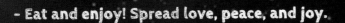

- Eat and enjoy! Spread love, peace, and joy.